_____*read this story for the first time*

on _____ _____*, 19*_____

First Edition
Printed in the U.S.A.
by
Taylor Publishing Company
1550 West Mockingbird Lane, Dallas, Texas 75235

ISBN 0-9636442-1-1

The Christmas Eve Tradition

As reported by
R. W. (Bob) Thompson, Jr.
and illustrated by
Roderick K. Keitz
and published by
The North Pole Chronicles

**"....... he asked that the whole thing be repeated
next Christmas Eve, and the Christmas Eve after that.**

It would be a new Christmas Eve tradition."

In Santa's village at the North Pole, there was a new young reindeer that had everyone excited. He was always elected the captain of the team, when he played in all the reindeer games.

The elves called him Rumble, since his antlers were so heavy that they caused his hooves to make a rumbling noise when he ran across the snow. They were taller and had more branches than those of any of the other deer.

And, they were growing bigger every day.

No one was at all surprised when Santa put a notice
on the workshop bulletin board that said,

Notice
Rumble will be
joining the team
that pulls my
sleigh Christmas
Eve. Santa

From the very first day he joined the team's practices,
the elves couldn't keep their eyes off of him.

Rumble was a new
Superstar!

But he soon started having problems.
His antlers had grown so big that they often made him trip.
    He would stumble, and fall down.

A clumsy little elf called Pout began to sing to himself,
"Rumble, Rumble, watch him stumble."

Pout stumbled a lot, too,
since he was born with two left feet.

    As each day passed,
Rumble's antlers grew bigger and bigger,
    matters got worse and worse,
        and Rumble stumbled more and more.
    He tried to be brave by getting up and saying,
        "If at first you don't succeed, fly, fly again."

But everyone thought that it would be too dangerous
For Santa to take Rumble with him on Christmas Eve.
He would probably cause a wreck.

When the official announcement saying that Rumble would stay
home was put on the bulletin board, Pout started singing out loud,
"Rumble, Rumble, watch him stumble."

And then he added,
    "He's no Rumble, he's a Stumble —
        Stumble, Stumble, Stumble, Stumble."

Sadly, everyone called the young reindeer Stumble from then on.
He was never called Rumble again.

As Santa climbed aboard his sleigh on Christmas Eve,
he paused to wave to Stumble.
He knew his heart must be breaking right then.

"It would have been too dangerous to take him," Santa thought.

"His antlers have grown so big and have so many branches that he
looks like one of those things kids climb on in a school yard.

He's a walking jungle gym!"

Then Santa shouted those familiar words,
"Now Dasher, Now Dancer, Now Prancer . . . . ."

When Santa left on his trip around the world,
only a teary-eyed Stumble was still outside to watch.
Then he, too, started back to the barn to join all
of the other reindeer who had been left behind.
He didn't even notice that the tips of the runners on Santa's sleigh
had caught a string of Christmas tree lights,
and carried them up into the sky.

When he came near the workshop where the elves had gathered,
Stumble wondered why he heard nothing but moans, groans,
gripes, and "boy, am I tired" talk from inside.

"This should be their happiest night of the year," he thought,
"They should be proud knowing that they had finished making
all of the toys Santa needed. They had done their share."

Stumble knew he had only been a disappointment.

It was then that one of the reindeer's hooves
hit the string of Christmas tree lights
that were hanging down from Santa's sleigh,
and they fell to the ground below.

They landed on Stumble's antlers,
just as he passed the workshop door.

The lights didn't weigh very much,
but they were all it took to make Stumble stumble through the door,
and onto the floor in front of all the elves.

What a sight! What a mess! What an unexpected surprise!

The elves stopped their griping, groaning, and complaining,
and started laughing at poor Stumble.

But Pout felt sorry for the former hero.

He went over and plugged in the lights
that had fallen onto Stumble's antlers,
and said, "Let there be light!"

Then Captain Horatio Oldsalt, the elf
in charge of making all of Santa's sea toys,
came over and changed the light on the
farthest left antler to a flashing red one.

He changed the light on the farthest right antler
    to a flashing green one.

"Now you can tell which way Stumble is going,"
    said the old sea captain,
"just like you can tell which way a boat or an airplane is going
    when you see their red and green lights."

Pout took an ornament from a nearby Christmas tree,
and put it on the brightly-lighted antlers.
The other elves started laughing even louder that before.

They took more ornaments off the tree,
and put them on Stumble.

A small grin appeared on Stumble's face.
He shook his head,
the lights and ornaments that covered his antlers shook, too.

Then he slowly stood up.

When his huge set of newly-decorated antlers reached high above
everything in the room, he started singing,
"Oh Christmas tree, oh Christmas tree.
It's really Stumble, can't you see."

The elves joined hands·and danced around the Stumble "tree."

Everyone joined in the fun.

When Santa came back, he was so pleased to see everyone happy
That he asked that the whole thing be repeated
next Christmas Eve, and the Christmas Eve after that.

It would be a new Christmas Eve tradition.

Christmas Eve had become the happiest night of the year.

But it wouldn't have
if Stumble hadn't stumbled into the room.

In future issues,
The North Pole Chronicles will tell you
about some of the exciting things that
happen to the North Pole elves
at other times of the year.

For example, *The Shopping Trip* is about
Santa's spring trip around the world to look
for new toys, and *The 4th of July Parade*
tells how a new patriotic symbol is created.

I hope you enjoy reading them as much as
I enjoy reporting them.

R. W. (Bob) Thompson, Jr.